BABES in TOYLAND

Retold by Gina Shaw • Illustrated by John Speirs

SCHOLASTIC INC.

Cartwheel BOOKS®

New York Toronto London Auckland Sydney

To Brian, Matt R., Matt S., and Jeff
—G.S.

To Siggy and Tilly,
and all my young friends
—J.S.

ISBN 0-590-48183-5

Text copyright © 1994 by Scholastic Inc.
Illustrations copyright © 1994 by John Speirs.
All rights reserved. Published by Scholastic Inc.
CARTWHEEL BOOKS is a registered trademark of Scholastic Inc.

12 11 10 9 8 7 6 5 4   5 6 7 8 9/9

Printed in the U.S.A.   24

First Scholastic printing, October 1994

"Come, children! Gather 'round! Help me prepare the village square!" called Mother Goose. Her children raced from all directions.

Jack and Jill came down from the hill. Little Miss Muffet jumped up from her tuffet. Little Bo Peep stopped counting her sheep. Their other brothers and sisters came running, too.

It was the day before Christmas Eve. The children were very excited. They all wanted to help decorate Mother Goose Village for their favorite holiday!

Some children hung garlands of holly and berries on the tall Christmas tree.

Others hammered green, red, and gold wreaths on all the doors.

And some placed small wooden toys on the branches of the tree. What better way for Mother Goose Village, the largest town in Toyland, to celebrate Christmas than with tiny toys!

Contrary Mary, Mother Goose's oldest daughter, placed a bright star at the top of the tree. This was an extra-special time for her. On Christmas Day, she would marry her true love, Tom Piper. Mary's smile matched the brightness of the star.

But just as she was on her way down from the ladder, a dark cloud seemed to cover the village. Everyone gasped....

It was Barnaby, the richest, greediest, and most powerful man in Toyland. He was very unhappy. He did not want Mary to marry Tom. He wanted to marry her himself!

Barnaby had a plan, and he was about to put it into action.

"Clear the square!" bellowed Barnaby. "Christmas will *not* be celebrated this year! Take down these decorations."

Barnaby turned to Mother Goose and said, "As of today, I am charging you double your rent."

Mother Goose could not believe her ears. Then Barnaby said, "But maybe we can make a deal. Call off the wedding and you can live here rent free!"

"Tom and Mary love each other," said Mother Goose. "We can't stop their wedding."

Barnaby turned away muttering, "We'll see about that!"

Barnaby's sidekick, Roderigo, found Barnaby as he was walking home. "I took care of everything," said Roderigo. "We'll get rid of Tom tonight."

Mary heard Roderigo and Barnaby talking, and she stopped them.

"What are you planning to do to Tom?" she demanded.

"My only plans are the plans for our wedding," Barnaby said slyly.

Mary wanted to get far away from these two men. She wanted to find Tom. She ran and ran without looking where she was going. The news that Mary had run away spread quickly. It even reached Tom.

Mary did not know that Barnaby and Roderigo came after her. They followed her into the deepest, darkest, and most dangerous place in all of Toyland — the Forest of No Return!

Soon the forest worked its spell on all of them, and they fell fast asleep. As they slept, gigantic spiders came out of hiding. The spiders spun silken webs tightly around each of them.

As the spiders scurried away, Tom entered the forest looking for Mary. He gasped when he saw her. Tom knelt beside Mary and gently brushed a moth from her shoulder.

Suddenly the moth fluttered its wings and changed into a beautiful butterfly. It untangled the spiderweb and lifted both Tom and Mary onto its back. Then it carried them safely out of the Forest of No Return to the doorstep of the Toymaker.

Inside the Toymaker's shop, the Toymaker and his assistant, Grumio, were very busy indeed. They had to make all the Christmas toys for the boys and girls of Toyland. These two loved to tinker. Right now they were busy working on a machine that could bring toys to life!

Grumio flipped the power switch on. The great machine sputtered. A large doll came down the assembly line. Smoke was pouring out of it.

The Toymaker scratched his head. "If at first you don't succeed, Grumio, try, try again!"

Just then Mary and Tom raced into the workshop.

Grumio was joyous. "Look! Our dolls *are* coming to life!" he said.

Mary pleaded with the Toymaker. "Won't you help us? Old Barnaby is spreading unhappiness everywhere. He's trying to

stop the village Christmas celebration and our wedding!"

The wise old Toymaker said, "Don't worry! Nothing bad can happen to you here. Now pretend you are my dolls and line up with the other toys."

Tom and Mary did just what the Toymaker told them to do.

At that moment Barnaby and Roderigo burst into the Toymaker's workshop. "I know Tom and Mary are here," Barnaby shouted. "Where are they?" Then the toy machine caught his eye.

"What have we here?" he asked, walking toward the machine. The Toymaker answered, "This machine makes toys!"

"Then I will make lots of toys for myself," Barnaby said with a greedy smile. He began flicking switches and turning knobs.

Suddenly toys came off in all directions, and they were coming to life! The Toymaker's machine was working after all!

"Now is your chance," whispered the Toymaker to Tom and Mary. "Lead the toys and scare Barnaby and Roderigo away."

And that is what they did! Barnaby couldn't believe the toys were alive. When he saw them, he screamed and ran.

Barnaby and Roderigo ran until they reached the edge of Toyland. As they crossed the border, Tom, Mary, and all the toys began to cheer, for everyone knows that once you pass the borders of Toyland, you can never return again.

Tom and Mary went back to the workshop, and all of the toys followed. One by one, they became regular toys again.

Tom and Mary thanked the Toymaker. He gave them lots of toys to take back for the children in Mother Goose Village.

Then he said, "Have a very Merry Christmas! Always keep love in your heart."

Finally it was Christmas Day.
Tom and Mary's wedding was beautiful.

And all the children had a wonderful time celebrating Christmas in Mother Goose Village!